P9-APN-255

For Aunt Vin
—remembering all those great Eberhart reunions.

Published 2008 by Concordia Publishing House
3558 S. Jefferson Avenue
St. Louis, MO 63118-3958
1-800-325-3040 • www.cph.org

Text © 2008 Dandi Daley Mackall

Illustrations © 2008 Concordia Publishing House

All rights reserved. No part of this publication may be reproduced,
stored in a retrieval system, or transmitted, in any form or by any means,
electronic, mechanical, photocopying, recording, or otherwise,
without the prior written permission of Concordia Publishing House.

Manufactured in China

1 2 3 4 5 6 7 8 9 10   17 16 15 14 13 12 11 10 09 08

That's My Colt
An Easter Tale

Written by Dandi Daley Mackall

Illustrated by Chris Ellison

CONCORDIA PUBLISHING HOUSE • SAINT LOUIS

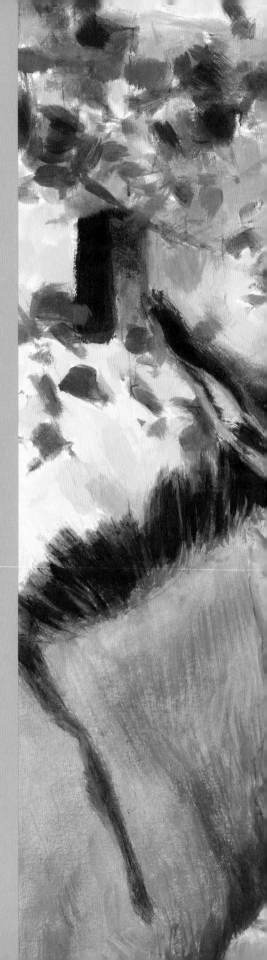

$\mathcal{I}$ had long cared for my father's donkey in our village of Bethphage. As I tied old Vashti and gazed across the Mount of Olives, I dreamed of owning my own donkey.

"When you are old enough, Matthias," my father promised, "I will give you a colt."

My father kept his word and gave me Vashti's last foal on my tenth birthday. I named my colt Abner and brushed his coat until his big eyes drooped.

"One day," I whispered into his long, soft ears, "we will gallop all over Jerusalem."

With my care and the Lord's blessing, my colt grew. I longed to train him to ride, but my mother kept me busy with preparations for the Passover.

"We must bake our unleavened bread, Matthias," Mother explained, "to remind us that our people left Egypt in a hurry. When God sent Moses to deliver us from slavery, we had no time for our bread to rise. And there is no time for you to train your colt."

We were gathered at table, when loud voices rose from the street below. Our neighbor shouted out to us, "Come quickly! They're taking your animals!"

I was the first to reach the courtyard. Two men were untying our donkeys. "Stop!" I cried. "That's *my* colt!"

"*W*hy are you untying that colt?" my father demanded.

The younger man answered, "The Master has need of it."

We knew the Master, Jesus. We had listened to Him beside the sea. Once, I saw Him heal a man who had been born blind.

Father turned to me and nodded. With a pain in my soul, I let go of my colt.

I watched them lead away my Abner and listened until the *clip-clop* of his hooves faded. *It's not fair!* I thought. *Abner is mine.*

I waited until my father and the others drifted back inside, then I set out after my colt.

When I caught up with them, Jesus was scratching Abner's ears, exactly like I always did. One of the men put his cloak on Abner's back. The colt sidestepped.

With horror, I realized Jesus was planning to ride my donkey. "Wait!" I cried, springing from my hiding place. "Abner has never been ridden!"

Jesus grinned over at me. Then He climbed onto Abner's back, and the colt grew as calm as old Vashti.

mazed, I trailed along as Jesus rode toward Jerusalem. Crowds were waiting in the city. They tossed their cloaks on the ground before Jesus and waved palm branches.

"Hosanna!" they cried. "Blessed is He who comes in the name of the Lord!"

And through it all, my unbroken colt carried the Master.

I faded into the crowd, so proud of Abner. Yet I grieved for my loss. Why hadn't the Master chosen a white stallion or a Roman chariot instead of my little colt? For hours, I walked the hills, alone with my memories of Abner.

The sun was setting as I returned home. And there, in the last light of day, I saw two donkeys. "Abner!" I cried. My colt had been returned to me.

*T*he week passed, filled with Passover preparations. We were retiring for the night when our neighbor burst in with terrible news. "They've arrested Jesus! There are plans to kill Him. All Jerusalem is in an uproar!"

I was not the only one to cry that night. Why would anyone want to kill the Master?

Sleep would not come to me, and by morning I knew what I had to do. I waited for my parents to leave our house. Then I untied Abner and headed for Jerusalem. I would let Jesus ride my colt far away to safety.

s soon as I entered the city, I knew something terrible had happened. Women were crying in the street. People streamed down from the hill to Golgotha.

Suddenly, the sky turned black. The wind tore at the earth. People screamed. It felt like the end of the world. As lightning sliced the sky, I looked toward Golgotha. Three crosses stood on the hill.

And in the center was Jesus, crucified. Dead.

*F*or days, I refused to leave my bed.
I felt, in some way, it was my fault. Maybe,
if I hadn't been so selfish. . . .

"Matthias! Come!" There was some-
thing in my mother's voice. Joy?

My father knelt at my side. "Matthias!
He is alive! The Master, Jesus, has risen
from the tomb!"

I climbed onto Abner's back, and off we raced to Jerusalem. Abner didn't stop until he reached the tomb in the garden. A young woman stood nearby.

"Is it true?" I called to her.

"It's true!" she cried. "Jesus Christ has risen from the dead!"

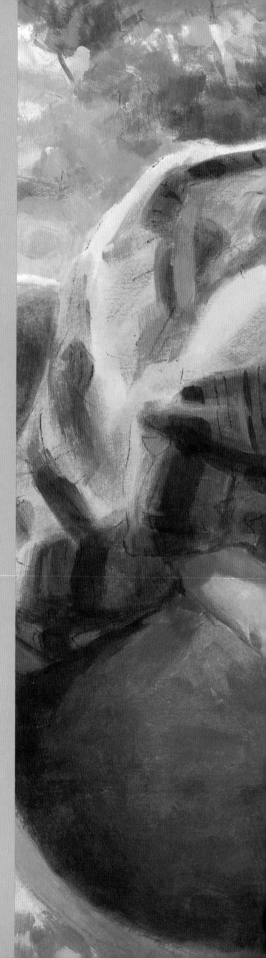

bner's mane flew, tickling my cheeks, making me laugh. The Master had ridden here on my colt. Now, I galloped through the city, on *our* colt, shouting the good news: "Hallelujah! He lives!"